To Jake, Rory and Taylor, Love Dad.

Newport Publishers, Incorporated, Laguna Niguel, California 92667
Newport Publishers and the portrayal of the sailboat are trademarks of Newport Publishers, Incorporated.

LET'S GO HIPPO
© 1992 Kingdom Resources, Inc./Toucan Productions
Written by Kenneth Hayes
Illustrated by Don Sullivan

Typesetting, Karen Heydman, LaserWriting, Inc.
Dust jacket Photography, Howard Sokol, Denver.

All rights reserved. No part of this publication may be reproduced, stored in a retrieval system, or transmitted, in any form or by any means, electronic, mechanical, photocopying, recording or otherwise, without prior permission of the publisher.

96 95 94 93 92   5 4 3 2 1
Printed in Hong Kong.   Published 1992.

Publisher's Cataloging in Publication Data

Hayes, Kenneth B.
    Let's Go Hippo

ISBN: 1-56729-025-6 Hardcover. USA 14.95/16.95 CANADA

LET'S GO HIPPO

By Kenn Hayes

Illustrated by Don Sullivan

NEWPORT PUBLISHERS, INCORPORATED

LET'S GO HIPPO

NOT NOW COW

YOU'RE SWEET PARAKEET

I'M TRYIN' LION

YOU'RE SUNK SKUNK

WE WANNA IGUANA

TOO SOON RACCOON

THANKS A LOT OCELOT

GET
LOOSE
MONGOOSE

WE'RE GOLFIN' DOLPHIN

GOOD LUCK DUCK

YOU'RE FUNKY MONKEY

OF COURSE HORSE

YOU WISH FISH

JUST RIBBIN' GIBBON

THE
END
FRIEND